A Note from the Author

The idea for *Room on the Broom* came about when I started to think about witches and cats. Witches in storybooks, you see, are almost always accompanied by cats and, of course, the cats often ride with the witches on the backs of their broomsticks.

What would happen, I wondered, if a witch didn't just have a cat but lots of animals? Would they all travel with her? How would they all fit onto a broomstick? And how much weight can one broom carry? And that's where the basic storyline came from.

There wasn't a dragon in the original story, but once the broom had broken and everyone had tumbled to the ground I created him to add some more excitement and drama. And as to the trick that the animals play on the dragon to save the witch? Well, I think I must have been inspired by the story of "The Musicians of Bremen". "The Musicians of Bremen" is a German folktale about four old animals – a donkey, a dog, a cat and a rooster – who come across a band of robbers in a cottage in some woods. They climb on one another's backs and make a fearful din. The robbers are convinced that there must be a terrible creature outside and run away, leaving the animals to settle in for the evening. It's a wonderful story and I am indebted to it because, although it was unconscious at the time, I think it must have been an inspiration.

The witch herself though, is definitely based on me! I am quite scatty. When I was a child I was always dropping and losing things, just like the witch in *Room on the Broom*. In fact, I still do. I can remember seeing the first sketches that Axel drew of the witch and asking my editor if she could be made a bit younger and less tidy, and if her nose might be a bit smaller. She looked older, wartier and much neater than I'd thought of her when I was writing the story. But now, of course, I am extremely fond of the witch and couldn't imagine her looking any other way.

Julia Donaldson

August 2015

For Natasha, Sabrina and Jasmine – J.D.

First published 2001 by Macmillan Children's Books
This edition published 2016 by Macmillan Children's Books
an imprint of Pan Macmillan
20 New Wharf Road, London N1 9RR
Associated companies throughout the world
www.panmacmillan.com

ISBN 978-1-4472-8657-8

1 3 5 7 9 8 6 4 2

A CIP catalogue record for this book is available
from the British Library.

Printed in Italy

Room on the Broom

by Julia Donaldson

Illustrated by Axel Scheffler

MACMILLAN
CHILDREN'S BOOKS

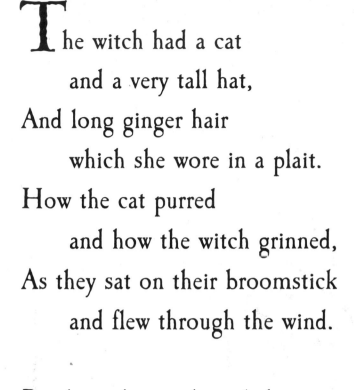

The witch had a cat
      and a very tall hat,
And long ginger hair
      which she wore in a plait.
How the cat purred
      and how the witch grinned,
As they sat on their broomstick
      and flew through the wind.

But how the witch wailed
      and how the cat spat,
When the wind blew so wildly
      it blew off the hat.

"Down!" cried the witch,
and they flew to the ground.
They searched for the hat
but no hat could be found.

Then out of the bushes
on thundering paws
There bounded a dog
with the hat in his jaws.

He dropped it politely,
   then eagerly said
(As the witch pulled the hat
   firmly down on her head),
   "I am a dog, as keen as can be.
   Is there room on the broom
      for a dog like me?"

"Yes!" cried the witch,
   and the dog clambered on.
The witch tapped the broomstick and
   whoosh! they were gone.

Over the fields and the
forests they flew.
The dog wagged his tail
and the stormy wind blew.
The witch laughed aloud
and held onto her hat,
But away blew the bow
from her long ginger plait!

Then out from a tree,
    with an ear-splitting shriek,
There flapped a green bird
    with the bow in her beak.
She dropped it politely
    and bent her head low,

"Down!" cried the witch,
    and they flew to the ground.
They searched for the bow
    but no bow could be found.

Then said (as the witch
    tied her plait in a bow),
"I am a bird,
    as green as can be.
Is there room on the broom
    for a bird like me?"

"Yes!" cried the witch,
    so the bird fluttered on.
The witch tapped the broomstick and
    whoosh! they were gone.

Over the reeds and the
rivers they flew.
The bird shrieked with glee
and the stormy wind blew.
They shot through the sky
to the back of beyond.
The witch clutched her bow
but let go of her wand.

"Down!" cried the witch,
and they flew to the ground.
They searched for the wand
but no wand could be found.

Then all of a sudden
    from out of a pond
Leapt a dripping wet frog
    with a dripping wet wand.
He dropped it politely,
    then said with a croak
(As the witch dried the wand
    on a fold of her cloak),
"I am a frog, as clean as can be.
Is there room on the broom
    for a frog like me?"
"Yes!" said the witch, so the frog
    bounded on.

The witch tapped the broomstick and
    whoosh! they were gone.
Over the moors and the
    mountains they flew.
The frog jumped for joy and . . .

. . . THE BROOM SNAPPED IN TWO!

Down fell the cat and the dog
and the frog.
Down they went tumbling
into a bog.

The witch's half-broomstick
flew into a cloud,
And the witch heard a roar
that was scary and loud . . .

"I am a dragon, as mean as can be,
And I'm planning to have WITCH
AND CHIPS for my tea!"
"No!" cried the witch,
   flying higher and higher.
The dragon flew after her,
   breathing out fire.
"Help!" cried the witch,
   flying down to the ground.
She looked all around
   but no help could be found.

The dragon drew nearer and,
   licking his lips,
Said, "Maybe this once
   I'll have witch without chips."

But just as he planned
  to begin on his feast,
From out of a ditch
  rose a horrible beast.
It was tall, dark and sticky,
  and feathered and furred.
It had four frightful heads,
  it had wings like a bird.
And its terrible voice,
  when it started to speak,
Was a yowl and a growl
  and a croak and a shriek.
It dripped and it squelched
  as it strode from the ditch,
And it said to the dragon,
  "Buzz off! –
  THAT'S MY WITCH!"

The dragon drew back
and he started to shake.
"I'm sorry!" he spluttered.
"I made a mistake.
It's nice to have met you,
but now I must fly."
And he spread out his wings
and was off through the sky.

Then down flew the bird
and down jumped the frog.
Down climbed the cat,
and "Phew!" said the dog.
And, "Thank you, oh, thank you!"
the grateful witch cried.
"Without you I'd be
in that dragon's inside."

Then she filled up her cauldron
and said with a grin,
"Find something, everyone,
throw something in!"
So the frog found a lily,
the cat found a cone,
The bird found a twig
and the dog found a bone.

They threw them all in
     and the witch stirred them well,
And while she was stirring
     she muttered a spell.
"Iggety, ziggety, zaggety, ZOOM!"

Then out rose . . .

...A TRULY MAGNIFICENT BROOM!

With seats for the witch
    and the cat and the dog,
A nest for the bird and
    a shower for the frog.

"Yes!" cried the witch,
    and they all clambered on.
The witch tapped the broomstick and
    whoosh! they were gone.

The witch looked quite different when Axel first started to draw her!

Her hat used to be much smaller.

In an early sketch, she wore a jacket instead of a cape.

At one point she had a green top and tights. What colour did they become?

She didn't have a wart on her nose.

Which witch do you prefer?